# TINY TED'S
# BIG ADVENTURE

Peter Bowman

*For Holly and Rory*

Tiny Ted woke up with a big yawn.
'Breakfast time,' said Mouse.

'It's so quiet here,'
sighed Tiny Ted.

'I wonder what it's
like out there.'

'Phew, that was
a tight squeeze ...'

'… Oh, what a lovely morning.
I think I'll have a little holiday.'

'This is perfect!'

'I can go sailing ...'

'... and sunbathing.'

'But, maybe there
isn't room for two.'

'Lucky I can swim.
Whoa, what's happening?'

'Oh thank you.
I think I'm safer
on dry land.'

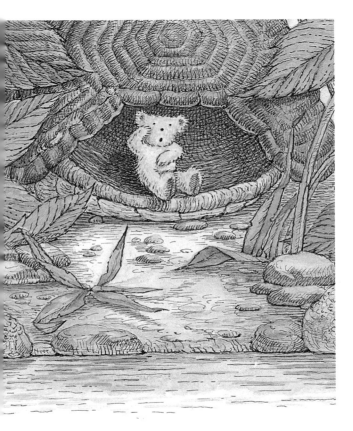

'Phew, it's getting hot. I'll
shelter for a while in this cave.'

'Whoops!'

'Mmm, this is nice and soft.
I'll just dry myself off.'

'Oh, excuse me. I thought
you were a powder puff.'

'Now I'm stuck, with no
one to rescue me.'

'Thank you. Country
people are very kind.'

'But how do I get down?'

'By whirligig,
of course!
Wheee!'

'Oh dear.
No more sun.'

'I think it's time to go home.'

'But which way?'

'Oh, help. I'm lost
and it's dark and
I'm very, very small.'

'There you are,' said Mouse.
'I'm glad I've found you.'

'So am I,' said Tiny Ted.
'I've had a big adventure.
But really ...'

'... there's no place like home.'

THE END

A TED SMART Publication 1997

First published in 1994

1 3 5 7 9 10 8 6 4 2

© Peter Bowman 1994

Peter Bowman has asserted his right under
Copyright, Designs and Patents Act, 1988,
to be identified as the author of this work

First published in the United Kingdom in 1994 by
Hutchinson Children's Books
Random House UK Limited
20 Vauxhall Bridge Road, London SW1V 2SA

Random House Australia (Pty) Limited
20 Alfred Street, Milsons Point, Sydney,
New South Wales 2061, Australia

Random House New Zealand Limited
18 Poland Road, Glenfield,
Auckland 10, New Zealand

Random House South Africa (Pty) Limited
PO Box 337, Bergvlei 2012, South Africa

Random House UK Limited Reg. No. 954009

Printed in China